WASHOE COUNTY LIBRARY

3 1235 03151 7464

MAY 1 1 2006

D0598371

Forgiving a Friend

Virginia Kroll

illustrated by **Paige Billin-Frye**

Albert Whitman & Company, Morton Grove, Illinois

The Way I Act Books:

Forgiving a Friend • *Jason Takes Responsibility*

The Way I Feel Books:

When I Care about Others • *When I Feel Angry*

When I Feel Good about Myself • *When I Feel Jealous*

When I Feel Sad • *When I Feel Scared* • *When I Miss You*

Kroll, Virginia L.
Forgiving a friend / written by Virginia Kroll ; illustrated by Paige Billin-Frye.
p. cm. — (The way I act)
Summary: Seth cannot forgive his friend Jacob for breaking a favorite toy until he learns first hand that
friends and family are more valuable than anything.
ISBN 0-8075-0618-4 (hardcover)
[1. Best friends—Fiction. 2. Forgiveness—Fiction. 3. Conduct of life.] I. Billin-Frye, Paige, ill. II. Title. III. Series.
PZ7.K9227For 2005   [E] — dc22 2005002743

Text copyright © 2005 by Virginia Kroll.
Illustrations copyright © 2005 by Paige Billin-Frye.
Published in 2005 by Albert Whitman & Company,
6340 Oakton Street, Morton Grove, Illinois 60053-2723.
Published simultaneously in Canada by Fitzhenry & Whiteside, Markham, Ontario.
All rights reserved. No part of this book may be reproduced or transmitted in any form or by any means, electronic or mechanical,
including photocopying, recording, or by any information storage and retrieval system, without permission in writing from the publisher.

Printed in the United States.
10 9 8 7 6 5 4 3 2 1

The design is by Carol Gildar.

For more information about Albert Whitman & Company,
please visit our web site at www.albertwhitman.com.

For Seth and Grandma Grace Meyers,
who always forgives—V.K.

"I'll race you!" Seth shouted as he and his best friend, Jacob, rode their bikes up and down the driveway.

"Ready, set, go!" Jacob yelled. "I'm the fastest!"

Suddenly, Seth heard a crash. Jacob, his bike, and Seth's shiny yellow dump truck were in a heap near the fence.

"Ow," said Jacob, rubbing his knee and dusting off his pants.

Seth didn't say, "Are you okay?" He said, "Hey, you broke my truck!"

Jacob said, "I'm sorry, Seth. I didn't mean it. It was an accident."

Seth scowled at Jacob and shouted, "That truck was brand-new, and now it's all smashed up. You get out and don't ever come back!"

Jacob sadly got on his bike and rode home.

Seth barged into the house with a forehead of angry lines. He told his mom what had happened. "I hate Jacob," he announced.

Mom said, "I'm really sorry about your truck, Seth. But what if you had broken one of his toys? Is that how you'd want Jacob to treat you?"

Seth stomped his foot. "Well, I didn't break his toy. He broke mine," he said. "Now I need a new truck *and* a new best friend."

The next day, Seth played alone. It wasn't as much fun as playing with Jacob, but Seth was still mad. He was glad when Mom said, "Seth, Grandma Grace made strawberry shortcake, and she wants us to help her eat it." Seth enjoyed going to his special neighbor's house.

After their yummy treat, Grandma Grace got out
the circus toys that she kept in the closet. Seth played
in the living room while Mom and Grandma Grace
talked in the kitchen.

"Ladies and gentlemen . . ." Seth loved pretending to be the ringmaster and the lion tamer. But uh-oh! Musa, the mischievous monkey was escaping. Now Seth would have to be a monkey catcher, too.

He chased Musa over the couch, around the coffee
table, and up onto the end table. "Gotcha!" Seth yelled.

CRASH! went Grandma Grace's stained glass
lamp. It shattered into pieces like a breakable rainbow.

Seth stared at the broken lamp. Oh, no!
Now Grandma Grace would hate him!

Mom and Grandma Grace rushed in. "Are you okay?" they gasped.

"I'm sorry. I didn't mean it. I was just playing. Musa got away, and I was trying to catch him." Seth felt like he was going to cry.

Grandma Grace folded Seth into a hearty hug and said, "Seth, honey, we all have accidents. I'm just glad you and Musa didn't get hurt." She plucked Musa from the pile of glass and handed him to Seth.

Seth said, "I'll give you all my piggy bank money."

Mom said, "I'll pay the rest. That lamp was valuable."

Grandma Grace said, "Nonsense! You will not. There's nothing I own that's more valuable than friendship."

Seth couldn't believe his ears. He had broken Grandma Grace's favorite lamp, and she wasn't even angry. She forgave him, just like that!

On the way home, Seth kept thinking about Grandma Grace's words, "we all have accidents" and "nothing's more valuable than friendship." He had been so mad at Jacob. Maybe Jacob already had another best friend!

"Mom, I'm going to Jacob's, okay?" he said.

His mother smiled. "Good idea."

Seth wished he hadn't been so angry
with Jacob yesterday. Would Jacob forgive
him now? Well, there was only one way
to find out.

Seth took a deep breath. Then he
knocked loudly at Jacob's door.